Jun 2019

To David Streen, snake fart expert. This book would not have been possible without you.
—NC & DR

For Freya.
—AG

Little, Brown and Company
Hachette Book Group
1290 Avenue of the Americas, New York, NY 10104
Visit us at LBYR.com

First Edition: July 2019

Little, Brown and Company is a division of Hachette Book Group, Inc.
The Little, Brown name and logo are trademarks of Hachette Book Group, Inc.

The publisher is not responsible for websites (or their content) that are not owned by the publisher.

Library of Congress Cataloging-in-Publication Data • Names: Caruso, Nick, author. | Rabaiotti, Dani, author. | Griffiths, Alex G, illustrator. •
Title: Does it fart? : a kid's guide to the gas animals pass / Nick Caruso and Dani Rabaiotti ; illustrated by Alex G. Griffiths. • Description:
First edition. | New York ; Boston : Little, Brown and Company, [2019] | Originally published in U.S. in longer version, with a different
illustrator: New York : Hachette Books, [2018]. | Audience: Ages 4-8. • Identifiers: LCCN 2018050078| ISBN 9780316491044
(hardcover) | ISBN 9780316491228 (ebook) | ISBN 9780316491235 (library edition ebook) • Subjects: LCSH: Animal behavior—
Juvenile literature. | Flatulence—Juvenile literature. • Classification: LCC QL751.5 .C3575 2019 | DDC 591.5—dc23 •
LC record available at https://lccn.loc.gov/2018050078

ISBNs: 978-0-316-49104-4 (hardcover), 978-0-316-49122-8 (ebook), 978-0-316-49124-2 (ebook), 978-0-316-49121-1 (ebook)

About This Book

The illustrations for this book were done in pen and ink, and using Photoshop for the color treatment and texture. This book was edited by
Deirdre Jones and designed by Jen Keenan and Véronique Lefèvre Sweet. The production was supervised by Erika Schwartz, and the
production editor was Andy Ball. The text was set in Brandon Grotesque, and the display type is Billy Bold.

PRINTED IN CHINA

1010

10 9 8 7 6 5 4 3 2 1

Does It Fart?

A KID'S GUIDE
TO THE GAS ANIMALS PASS

Nick Caruso & Dani Rabaiotti • illustrated by **Alex G. Griffiths**

LITTLE, BROWN AND COMPANY
New York   Boston

This is a book about farts.

That's right. **Farts**. Otherwise known as **toots**. **Rips**. **Stinkers**. **Butt burps**.

Farts probably make you laugh, because a fart sound is funny! And a fart smell is even funnier—at least to some people. But where do these sounds and smells come from?

One answer is that when you eat and drink, you swallow little gulps of air along with the food and liquid. This air eventually comes back out, usually as burps, but sometimes as farts.

Another answer is that, as your body breaks down the food you eat in a process called *digestion*, it creates gas, which starts to build up in your stomach and intestines and needs to escape! So your muscles push the gas out as a fart, the same way it pushes out a poop. If you've ever heard someone say the words "pass gas," this is what they're talking about.

A third answer is that your body has super tiny creatures living inside it called *bacteria*, and when you eat a food that's hard to break down, the bacteria take care of it for you. They munch the food up and in the process make a lot of gas, which—you guessed it—comes out as farts.

You've probably noticed that there are different types of farts, some smellier than others, some more frequent than others. It all depends on the foods you eat, how healthy you are, and how much bacteria live in your gut.

For instance, if you eat vegetables like broccoli, beans, or peas, or if you eat dairy products like milk or yogurt, you'll probably find yourself farting up a storm. Plants and milk are made of materials

that take a long time to break down in your body, and the whole time they're breaking down, gas is building up.

Some farts don't smell too much, because they're mostly made up of an odorless molecule called *carbon dioxide*. But when you eat foods that have more sulfur in them, like meats, your farts will get seriously stinky. If you're sick or allergic to a food you eat, your body might make some smelly farts, too.

And sometimes you just have more bacteria living in your insides than other people do, and the best way to get rid of all the gas those little eating machines create is to force it out through your backside (making you a fartasaurus).

Are you laughing at how many times you've read the word *fart* already?

Good! Farts are funny, and if you have a dog at home, you know that animal farts are *super* funny. Think about it! A whale fart is probably HUGE, right? What about a snake? Or a spider? Can an octopus fart, and if it can, what comes out?

By the time you reach the end of this book, you'll know whether or not each of these animals passes gas (and you'll know more than you ever wanted to about *how* and *why* and *how much*):

Horse	**Ferret**	**Sea Lion**	**Lemur**
Parrot	**Beaded**	**Chimpanzee**	**Dog**
Cheetah	**Lacewing**	**Unicorn**	**Dinosaur**
Spider	**Goat**	**Snake**	**Herring**
Whale	**Salamander**	**Octopus**	**Kids**

Do you think you can guess which ones fart and which ones don't?

Let's find out. . . .

This is a horse.

Does it fart?

Yes!

It takes horses a long time to digest all the plants they eat, because plants are made of a substance called *cellulose*, which can be hard to break down. So horses' bodies have plenty of bacteria inside them to help. Lots of plants + lots of bacteria = lots and lots of farts. Horses are one of the most frequent farters in the animal kingdom.

This is a **parrot**.

Does it fart?

No!

Birds don't fart, because they don't have gas-making bacteria in their guts, and food passes too quickly through their bodies to allow gas to build up. Parrots are particularly good at mimicking sounds, though, which is why many people *think* they've heard a parrot fart. But they're actually just making the sound with their throats, kind of like when you blow a raspberry.

This is a cheetah.

Does it fart?

Yes!

Cheetahs eat meat, usually animals like gazelles and impalas, and chowing down on meat means cheetah farts come out really, really, really, *really* smelly. Maybe that's why they're the fastest land animal on the planet—they're trying to outrun the stink!

This is a spider.

Does it fart?

Nobody knows!

What scientists *do* know is that spiders eat only liquids. So when a spider bites its prey, it pushes venom into the body of its victim. Then the spider waits for the insides to break down into liquid so it can slurp up its dinner. (Gross!) Spiders do have bacteria in their bodies, though, and that bacteria might make gas, which means spiders *might* fart. (And you *might* want to throw up right about now.)

This is a whale.

Does it fart?

Yes!

Whales are enormous, and blue whales are the biggest animals on the planet! They have gigantic stomachs full of bacteria to break down foods like plankton or fish, and a whole lot of gas builds up as this happens, making their farts very big and awfully smelly. And that's not all! After a whale dies, gas can still build up inside it, and its body can get so full that it *explodes* like a popped balloon!

This is a **ferret**.

Does it fart?

Yes!

Ferrets are sometimes surprised by their farts and look confused after a toot escapes. Don't ever scare one on purpose, though, because when a ferret is frightened, it will scream, puff itself up, fart, and poop all at the same time (which will probably make you start screaming, too).

This is a beaded lacewing.

And this is a *baby* beaded lacewing.

Does it fart?

Yes!

Beaded lacewings lay their eggs on rotting wood right next to termite nests. When the baby bugs hatch, they sneak into the nest so they can eat the termites living inside! One species in particular kills the termites by—can you believe it?—*farting* on them. The beaded lacewing baby raises its tail and pushes out a chemical that makes a termite unable to move and eventually kills it. Then the bug baby chows down, all thanks to a genuinely *deadly* fart.

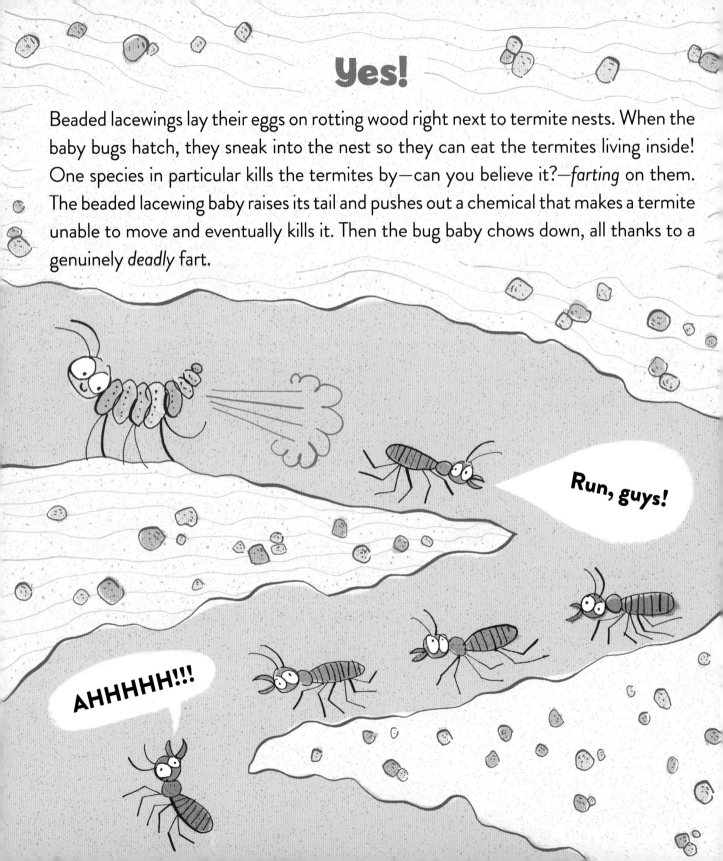

This is a **goat**.

Does it fart?

Yes!

Goats have four stomachs full of bacteria, and they eat mostly plants, both of which makes them fart a *lot*. And they burp even *more*. One time an airplane carrying two thousand goats had to land because all the farting (and burping) on board set off a fire alarm!

This is a **salamander**.

Does it fart?

Maybe...

No one has ever heard a salamander fart, so scientists' best guess is that they probably don't have strong enough muscles in their butts to push gas out and make a farting noise. Salamanders do poop on other animals when they think they're being attacked, though, and this poop can be super stinky. So don't make any sudden moves if you have a salamander for a pet.

I've got a little surprise for you. . . .

This is a **sea lion.**

Does it fart?

Yes!

Sea lions eat mostly fish (although some eat crabs or even penguins!), so their farts are particularly fishy and—you guessed it—super-duper smelly. Zookeepers have reported that sea lions have the stinkiest farts in the entire animal kingdom! So remember to pinch your nose the next time you visit them at the zoo.

This is a chimpanzee.

Does it fart?

Yes!

Chimpanzees fart loudly and often. Scientists have even used the sound of their farts to find them hiding in the wild! So the next time you want to play hide-and-go-seek, challenge a chimpanzee. You'll probably win.

This is a unicorn.

Does it fart?

Unicorns don't exist.

But if they did, YES! Unicorns are similar to horses, and horses fart a ton. So if unicorns existed, they would probably fart, and rainbows and glitter and cupcakes would probably come out with the gas.

This is a snake.

Does it fart?

Yes!

And that's not all. When this particular snake, a Sonoran coral snake, feels threatened, it hides its head under its body, raises its tail, sucks air into its cloaca (the part of a snake that poop and pee come out of), then forces the air back out in a burst to frighten predators. This makes a popping sound kind of like a higher-pitched, shorter version of a human fart. Not very scary, but definitely a neat trick.

**Be afraid.
Be very
afraid.**

This is an **octopus**.

Does it fart?

No!

Octopuses don't have the right bacteria in their bodies to create gas for farts. But they can do two things that are kind of like farting: 1) They can push water out of their bodies really quickly to jet themselves away from danger. 2) They can squirt out ink to confuse (and sometimes poison) predators. Pretty cool, right?

This is a lemur.

Does it fart?

Yes!

And that's not all! Lemurs use many kinds of smells to communicate with one another. Ring-tailed lemurs in particular make a smelly substance that comes out of their wrists, and another smelly substance that comes out of their shoulders. Male ring-tailed lemurs mix these together and rub it on their tails, then wave their tails in the air to start "stink fights." (So gross. And so awesome.)

This is a dog.

Does it fart?

Yes!

Because so many people have dogs, scientists have looked for ways to reduce the frequency of their farts and to make them less smelly. They even developed a special dog coat that would collect the farts so people wouldn't have to smell them. While testing the coat, one scientist had to rank test farts on how bad they stunk! So the next time your parents ask you to do your chores, be glad the job of smelling your dog's toots isn't one of them.

What did I do to deserve this?

This is a dinosaur.

Does it fart?

Not anymore!

Dinosaurs have been extinct for millions of years. The only animals alive today that evolved from dinosaurs are birds, and birds don't fart. But there were so many different kinds of dinosaurs that it's a safe bet that at least some of them farted. (And those farts must have been GIGANTIC.)

This is a herring.

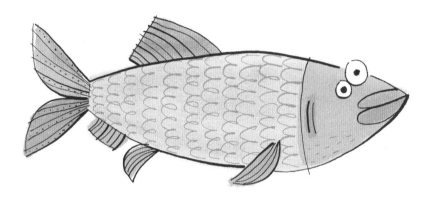

Does it fart?

Yes!

Herrings take big gulps of air from the surface of the water, store the air in their bodies, then push it out underwater in what's called a *fast repetitive tick*, or an FRT. (Ha!) FRTs are high-pitched raspberry-like sounds that last a few seconds, and scientists think herrings use the sounds to communicate and stay close to one another. The FRTs are too high-pitched for most predators to hear, so herrings basically have a secret fart code. (You're jealous—admit it.)

Hello to you, too!

These are some kids. Do they fart?

(You already know the answer to this one.)

Of course kids fart!

All humans do, from your parents to your neighbor to your teacher to the queen of England, and more! Humans fart around ten to twenty times each day (although some people fart as much as fifty times a day).

The funny thing is, humans are the only species on the planet who get embarrassed or grossed out by their farts. So take a cue from the animal kingdom the next time you accidentally let loose a toot: Remember that it's both funny *and* scientific, and everyone does it—including most of your favorite animals.

Just try not to start any stink fights. And *please* don't invent a secret fart code.